Traya's Quest
The Journey Begins

Paulette Agnew

Crystal Pointe Media, Inc. San Diego, CA

Traya's Quest
By Paulette Agnew

Copyright © 2015

Published 2015 by Crystal Pointe Media, Inc.
San Diego, California

ISBN-13: 978-0692511695
ISBN-10: 0692511695

This story is fiction and readers should not attempt to contact or come close to wild animals in any way. Children, when around animals and in the great outdoors, should always be supervised.

Cover Design and Illustrations by Timm Joy, UK

The Stardust Harmonies music by Tom Dicke | www.tomdicke.com

Dedication

Traya's Quest is dedicated with enormous love and gratitude to my mum and dad, Cynthia and Tom. Without them, I would not have had the amazing childhood I had. I lived in, played with and learned to love wild places, nature, mountains and animals. I am forever indebted to them both. What greater gift can you give a child than to take them safely into adulthood and to teach them to feel the Great Spirit by opening them up to the most beautiful playground we all share, Mother Earth?

Acknowledgements

They say it takes a community to raise a child; it also took one to bring Traya to the final stages of publication.

To all my spiritual and yogic friends, what a great journey we have had together discussing, exploring and embracing so much knowledge from the ancient texts and daily life. Thank you to Mansukh Patel, Chris Barrington and Louise Rowan on behalf of a very long list of incredible friends.

To my dear friends, who read, edited and reviewed *Traya's Quest* at different stages: Alison Peter, Asra Esmail, Christine Poland, Clodagh Whelan, Greg Carlin, Geraldine O'Donovan, Helen O'Neil, Kelly Molloy, Laura Murphy, Liselotte Hennekam, Mona Fairholme, Neil Cowmeadow, Paul and Vivi Ayres, Prof Gavin MacDonald, Robyn Schussing, Ruth Rohan Jones, Sally Pearson, Sean Kelly, Suzanna Thell and Sylvia Barrington. And thanks to all the young readers for your comments and feedback, including; Alex (10) and Lilly (7) in the UK and Rashid (10) in Dubai.

This adventure is set in Kenya, and my gratitude flows to those who welcomed and shared the very best of its secrets with me: Mandy Parkin, Simon and Roo Woods and especially Paul Krystall and his beautiful daughter, Aja.

Many thanks finally to my publishing and editing team for their guidance, encouragement and believing in me as an author: Jim DeBellis, Tina Erwin from Crystal Pointe Media publishing and Steve Harrison who helped me get Traya out of the cupboard.

Timm Joy's cover and illustrations are fabulous, thank you.

The Stardust Harmonies music by Tom Dicke adds a heavenly touch!

Thank you!

Foreword

It's not very often that I get blown away by a piece of fiction, but leave it to my globetrotting girlfriend to do just that. I'm not sure if Paulette is a spiritual mystic, an adventurer, a scientist or a philosopher, as she always has several diverse projects going on. Every time I run into her, whether it's in Mumbai, Los Angeles, London or Dubai, she always has an important and exciting discovery to share.

One of my favourite things about Paulette is that she never stops exploring and learning. She's one of those rare people who approaches life from a totally different angle, and then actually lives out her beliefs. She effortlessly integrates her acquired knowledge of nature and the world into her everyday life. Now she has incorporated this knowledge into an exciting new series of books, perfect for both kids and adults, *Traya's Quest*. Her first installment, The Journey Begins, follows a young boy who has the ability to commune, and communicate, with nature and animals as he searches for his purpose in life.

No one else could have written this book. The insights could only come from a person who herself lives life as a journey of discovery. Traya's motivation in life, like Paulette's, is a test of passion (something near and dear to my heart!).

I pride myself on connecting hearts to minds and minds to hearts, and this is what I love about Paulette Agnew's "Traya." For Paulette, and her perfectly portrayed character, heart and mind become one as they allow themselves to tune into their holistic essence and use the natural forces to guide them in their quest for purpose.

Traya's adventure teaches us that one's purpose in life is not found in a job or station in life, but rather in one's sense of motivation and the impact we make on the lives of others. A shoe shiner's purpose is not to shine shoes. It is to put confidence in a person's step, help them acquire gainful employment, allow them to feel the shine of their own dignity and let other people see them in the light of the respect they deserve.

Read this book to your young school-age children. Let your fifth graders tackle it on their own. Give it as a gift to your kids in high school and college. And read through it yourself in one sitting instead of watching TV.

As you do, I promise you'll feel your consciousness shift as you inject something very positive into your karmic bloodstream. This life on earth is precious, and Paulette's new book offers children of all ages something substantial and grounding that can help set them on a course towards a happy, fulfilling and heart-centred life.

Magic is on every page, and it's sure to rekindle the gift of living a life packed with purpose and powered by passion. This is what we need in our lives.

– Janet Bray Attwood,
Transformational Leader and Co-Author of the New York Times *Bestsellers,*
The Passion Test and Your Hidden Riches
www.thepassiontest.com

Contents

Chapter 1

The Question is Asked

Two million pink flamingos cried out together,

"What's your purpose, Traya?" as they filled the lake and sky with their shimmering and graceful shifting patterns of flight.

"Our purpose is to be beautiful, together as one. Watch us," the chorus of voices called, forming a new dazzling array of pink waves with their acrobatic displays. Meanwhile, the great white pelicans looked on with dignified detachment.

Traya looked out through wide brown eyes at wave after wave of pink feathers, swooping and rolling before landing gracefully in Lake Nakuru. A million stood, thousands flew and hundreds waded on tall, thin legs through the shallow lake, creating rainbows of colour on the surface, which reflected their beauty even more.

Eleven-year-old Traya clapped his hands with delight as the spectacle continued. He had been sitting there for hours watching the show with his best friend, Major, a boy from the local Maasai

tribe. Unlike Traya, Major couldn't understand what the flamingos were saying because that was Traya's special gift. He waited until Traya translated the endless honking into the Swahili dialect.

"*Jambo! Habari*," Major called out to the graceful birds. "Hello! How are you?" Instantly, as if in reply, nearly five hundred flamingos rose up in unison, stretched out their great wings and took off to perform a lap of honour.

"They like you!" Traya said and together the boys jumped up and waded a little way into the warm soda lake to get closer to their new friends. Though the flamingos told them it was safe from crocodiles, Major had his staff, knife and throwing stick tucked ready in his belt.

Traya turned to Major and said, "They are asking us what our purpose is, but they used the word *Dharma*. We have to find our *Dharma*. They explained that *Dharma* is not your actual job, but is more about why we are alive,how we choose to live each day in the highest way and our interaction with the rest of nature. They said it is called 'The Great Quest' and is the most important journey every person's soul needs to take.

"I'll need to think about it," Traya said to the flamingos, "but we promise we will come back and tell you as soon as we have found the answer to The Great Quest." Traya had dropped his voice into the gentle way he used when talking to the creatures and to nature around him.

As they turned to leave the lake, Traya slipped in the gurgling mud, landing flat on his face. Major roared with laughter at his friend's undignified position, and was joined by a nearby group of snooty, guffawing pelicans. They reached out their black-tipped wings and clapped them together.

"Yuck," gasped Traya, spitting out disgusting algae-filled water. "You eat this stuff?" The pelicans looked down their long yellow beaks at the sodden, swampy boy and smirked.

"Maybe your *Dharma* is to be dirty," one suggested.

"Or maybe you should be a swamp monster," sniggered another; and a third snorted, "His *Dharma* is to entertain us!" They waded off, leaving Major to pull Traya to his feet and away from the cacophony of discussions about his *Dharma*.

"We need to get home soon," Traya spluttered, while washing some slimy stuff off his teeth with water from his own bottle. "It will be dark in less than an hour."

They set off for the short run home, seeming to fly just above the ground as their feet matched each other stride for stride. The skin on the soles of their feet was thick and hardened like the deep red, sun-baked earth of Africa. Traya was lost in thought about the great question asked by the two million voices. Major thumped him on the back in fond farewell, and he grunted.

"*Kwaheri*," Traya panted. "Goodbye." He'd had to work hard to keep up with the taller Maasai boy, who seemed to have been born running.

"*Lala salama*," called out Major. "Sleep well." Major left his friend before reaching Traya's village. Even as the shadows lengthened and night began to fall, he still had one more hour to run before reaching his hut in the kraal. Major loved running in the night. His black skin merged into the darkness, making him almost invisible except for his red-checked blanket, bouncing over his back.

Traya stopped at the edge of the village and pumped water from the well over himself. He knew his mother would scold him if he came home stinking of pelican pooh and swamp mud. He ran his hands through the wild mop of hair and was almost dry by the time he reached the door of his hut.

"I'm home," he called and walked in to see that dinner, cooking on the open fire, was almost ready.

He loved the home they lived in. It was warm, safe and smelled of Indian spices, most often turmeric and coriander. He walked into the living area where some of the cooking was done on the fire. Pans and stainless steel bowls sat on the hearth, and a pile of sticks and dried cow dung

patties were stacked to one side. A simple table and four wooden chairs were placed to the left of the door, and an old sofa and one armchair sat before the fireplace. He knew he would curl up on the sofa later beside his mama and gaze into the dancing flames. Although he was quite grown up now, he still loved to join his father in his huge chair and feel his strong arms hold him close as they all talked about their day's activities. The walls at one time had been painted a pale blue, but much of that was peeling or faded. That only seemed to make it even more like their home.

"*Bundi*, my little owl," Traya's mother greeted him, using his pet name, "have you washed your hands?"

Chapter 2

Who is Traya?

Dattatraya, the son of Atri and Anasuya, much preferred to be called plain old Traya. His parents had longed and prayed for a child for many years back in India. Anasuya, whom everyone called Ana, taught dance and music to local children there, and Atri had worked happily in the local warehouse until a cyclone destroyed it and many jobs were lost.

Luckily, Atri's brother, who had a shop in Gilgil in Kenya and a promise of work, was able to send them money to get flights to start a new life in Africa.

They left their gentle tropical home on Pamban Island, in the Palk Strait between mainland India and Sri Lanka, and moved to the Great Rift Valley, near a beautiful lake and wild forest. Here Traya was born in a humble dwelling at midday, when the sun was at its zenith.

Traya's mother had always told him that it seemed as though the sun paused for one full minute that day to greet the new boy. A special ray of sunlight shone through the window, kissing him on the forehead, and for a moment the wind and sea were stilled in respectful silence. One by one the animals came to greet him—monkeys, elephants, lions, snakes, and even the giraffes

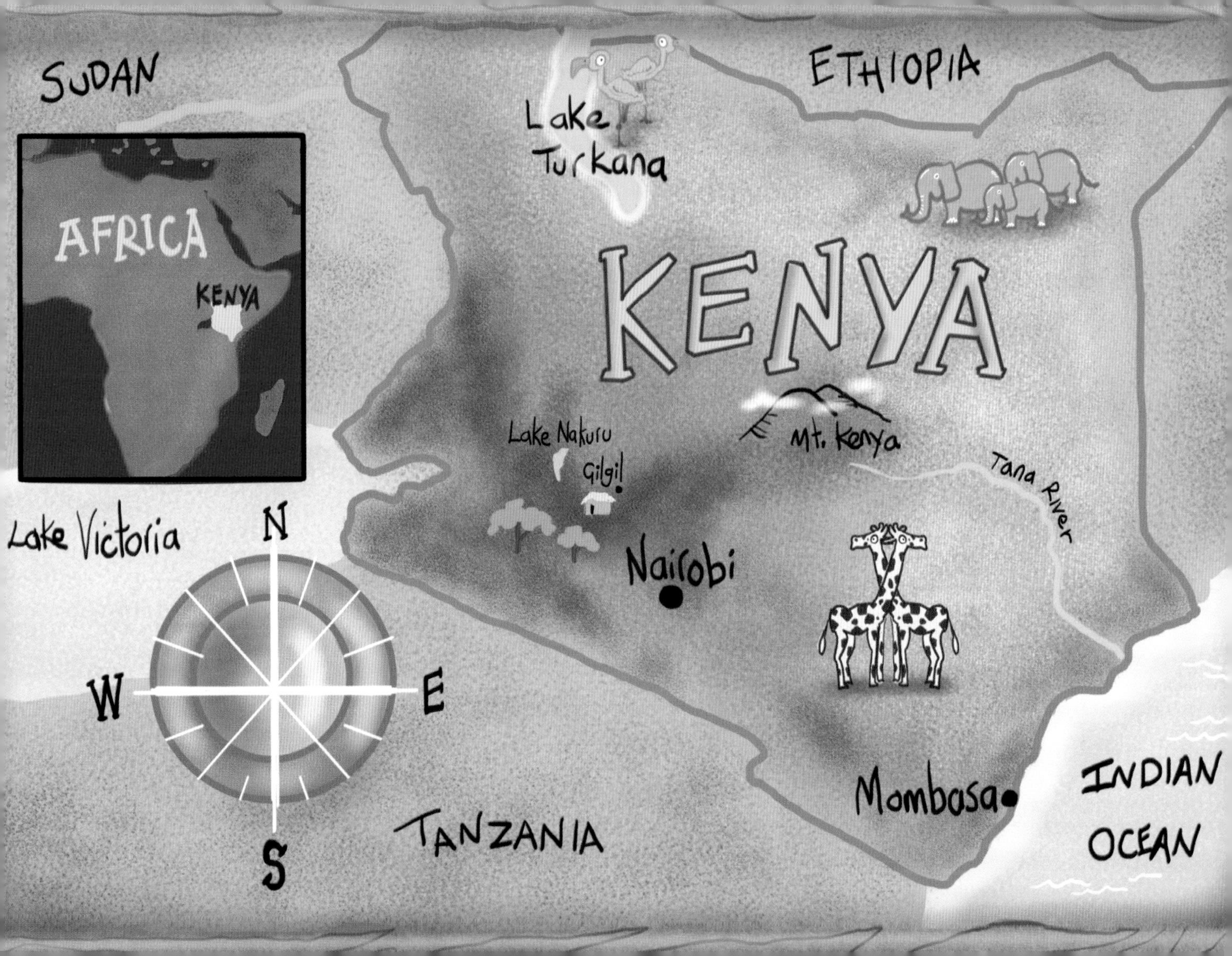
SUDAN
ETHIOPIA
Lake Turkana
AFRICA
KENYA
KENYA
Lake Nakuru
Gilgil
Mt. Kenya
Tana River
Lake Victoria
Nairobi
N
W
E
S
TANZANIA
Mombasa
INDIAN OCEAN

stuck their heads in to say hello; and little Traya seemed to be greeting them as well, waving his tiny baby fingers and chuckling with delight.

His loving and kind parents had all the time in the world for their special boy and, in their wisdom, they always encouraged Traya to do the things that felt right and natural to him. Ever since his birth, eleven years before, Traya had talked to the plants and animals, to the wind and the stars and to all natural things. He could talk to people as well, of course, but only he could hear the voices of the trees, the flowers, the bees and the lions; and they in turn could hear and understand him.

Although he was much smaller than his local village playmates, Traya was just as good at throwing sticks and chasing ostriches. Sometimes he even rode the ostriches if he could catch them and jump on their backs.

Traya did not go to school with his friends. His parents knew that he could learn much of what he needed to know from home-schooling and nature around him. Instead, he was free to wander in the wilderness, barefoot, feeling the warm earth between his toes. He spent his days watching the wild animals on the plains and forests and tracking them, and scrambling in the rugged hills. He loved to lie back sometimes with his arms outstretched, imagining himself to be one of the great birds of prey circling overhead, soaring on unseen currents of warm air. Every day was new

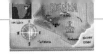

and unique, and he soon began to see how all the creatures and elements, beings and celestial bodies, worked together to make the world run in peace and harmony.

By the time he could walk, Traya also knew what the air and earth were saying to him, for they too were living parts of nature. Other children were busy playing games and trying to be better than each other. Traya knew that the natural world around him could teach him so much more.

He wondered what secrets the gigantic elephants kept hidden as they roamed past his house each day, and why the snakes whispered as they hid in the roof rafters of his humble home. Each day curiosity pushed him to find more answers. He discovered that the more answers he found, the more questions he had; naturally this made him eager to learn more and more. He understood that even the smallest and humblest creature had an important role in the web of life.

He kept these secrets to himself because he felt the other children would laugh at him. No one seemed to understand him, except perhaps his pet deer and the keeper of the beehives at the end of the dusty village road.

He was happy with his life. The sun had told him in a dream one day not to worry because he too would have a special job to do when he got older. So Traya grew up strong and sure of himself, happy and confident in his abilities, but aware of the differences between himself and other children.

The flamingos had really made him wonder about the special purpose that would come to define and give meaning to his life. The Great Quest beckoned him onwards.

"Mama," Traya asked his mother one day as he collected the banana peels from the breakfast table to take to the forest for the animals and insects to eat. "What is your special job, your purpose?"

"My special, job, Traya?" she asked with a sweet and twinkling smile. Ana was wearing her old work sari that day, as she had planned to wash the windows and remove the many wasp nests that seemed to decorate the walls with three dimensional mud sculptures. Her sari was cream and white, with a delicate emerald trim. It swished around her feet as she glided over the floor, and her ankle bells tinkled.

She had a matching short green blouse, showing her tummy and, as is the fashion, tightly fitted sleeves around her strong upper arms. The end of the sari was gathered over her left shoulder and draped down behind her back. She had tied her long black hair into a tight plait, which swished with the sari cloth as she worked. Traya loved to hear her moving around the house when he was pretending to sleep in the mornings. He would leap out of bed when he heard her bells as she walked towards his room.

"Yes, Mama," Traya continued thoughtfully. "The flamingos asked me if I knew my purpose. They said that every creature and every part of nature has a special job to do, in order to keep nature balanced and happy. I wondered what your special job is."

"Ah, I see, Traya. You are talking about The Great Quest. We call it our *Dharma*. It is our special purpose that makes us unique, different from all other people and creatures. My *Dharma* is to care for you and your father; to make sure that you grow big and strong and wise, and that your father stays strong in body, mind and spirit so that he can do his work every day. Most of all, I like to make other people healthy and happy. There are also many other things that I do that are part of my *Dharma*."

Traya nodded slowly, but he was confused. "But, Mama, isn't that what all mothers and teachers do? I thought that everyone's *Dharma* was special and different."

Ana smiled and stroked the back of her son's head. "You are very wise, Traya, which is why I call you my little owl. Your *Dharma* is not only what you do or give, but it is the whole chain of events that you put into the world."

Traya still looked confused, so she continued. "If your *Dharma* is to sing, then your singing will make vibrations in the air, and those vibrations may tickle the wings of a honey bee and help him put more joy into the honey he makes, and then later you will enjoy the honey even more and send some joy to Major and the flamingos, and it keeps on going, making the world a little better and happier each time."

Traya nodded slowly. "I guess I see…"

"Traya," Ana said, "you know the way you feel when I care for you and when you're with me?"

This time Traya's eyes lit up. He replied. "Ah! Nobody else, none of the animals – not even the Sun makes me feel that same way. You know just the right way to care for me and you fill up a part of me that no one else can! And then I bring that feeling to the animals and back to you too!"

Ana smiled and kissed Traya's forehead.

But, now that he had found this one answer, several more questions arose in him.

Finding an answer is like planting the maize that grows and produces more seeds that then need to be planted, he thought. One question makes more questions arise.

"So, Mama," he said slowly and thoughtfully, after a long pause, "you are the happiest person I know! Does that mean we all feel happy when we find our *Dharma*, our unique purpose?"

"That's a good question Traya," she replied. "Yes. I think it does."

"So what is my *Dharma*, Mama?" he asked.

"That is for you to discover in your journey through life as you explore your own unique strengths and gifts," she answered as she brushed his hair back with her fingers and began massaging his scalp.

Traya was lost in thought for the rest of the day's wanderings. *I must find my Dharma, he thought. How can I live my life properly and contribute to the benefit of nature if I don't even know why I'm here?*

His mind was far away as he watched their little family of goats grazing over the scrub and the crickets hopping though the long grass.

All these creatures, the grass, the trees and these great waters are following their purpose. They know and understand their Dharma. Maybe they can help me find mine.

Chapter 3

The Great Quest Begins

Traya was very quiet at dinner and went to his room to sleep much earlier than he normally did. He was proud of his small space and tried to keep it tidy, usually unsuccessfully. His bed was old and rickety, made from wood and lashed together with rope. The mattress was a bit lumpy, but Traya thought he was in paradise, as many of his friends didn't have one and slept on a rug on the floor.

He curled up in such a way that he avoided the metal springs which poked up through the coarse linen mattress and relaxed under his threadbare blanket. Their village was over 1700m above sea level, making the nights chilly, despite the burning heat of the day. Sleep did not come easily that night. He tossed and turned until it was time to get up at his usual time, two hours before sunrise. His father had told him this was a mystical and sacred time called Brahma Muhurta, a time when the veil between this world and the next was very thin. He had told Traya that most people were asleep at this time and missed this window of opportunity to connect with the angelic realms. Traya quickly did his chores, milked the goat and gathered the eggs from the chicken coop to put them on the table for his mother, but all the time The Great Quest to find his *Dharma* niggled at him.

I will go to the top of the nearby hill, he thought, and I will be the first one to greet the Sun when it meets the sky. Then he will see me and I'll ask him what my Dharma is. Traya ran across the plain and began to climb. Dawn had not yet chased away the darkness when he picked some berries and nuts for the mountain birds and insects, dropping them into a small bag he had filled with snacks and tied to his belt.

He stopped to look out over the vast valley, a great rift torn in the earth millions of years ago. Traya could only see a tiny fraction of the huge trench, 6000km long, stretching between Jordan in Asia and Mozambique in Southeast Africa. A mile away, he saw a huge herd of elephants drifting in and out of the predawn mist, like phantoms. They walked with dignity towards some unseen destination, stirring up clouds of dust in the still morning air. He looked back towards his house but could not find it in the haze. He would have to hurry to get to the summit before the sun poked its head above the horizon.

From the summit he saw the great Sun rising in the east, huge and red, spilling its life-giving warmth over all creation. Traya sat in silent reverence, watching until it became too bright for his dark brown eyes. He shaded his eyes with his hand, and felt the rays of light pouring into his head like melted ghee. Every cell of his body tingled with exhilaration and warmth.

He chanted the Gayatri mantra. His mother had taught him that it would bring light into his heart and mind on waking up. Traya then said to his friend the sun, "Hello, Surya. How are you?

Habari yako?" He thanked Surya for being with him in each moment. He then waited to hear what answer his friend might give him. He could always sense Surya's attention and approval, but he had never heard real answers before.

Since Traya was a small child, his daily practice had been to speak with the Sun, and he had learned to hear some very beautiful things, sometimes mysterious and sometimes mundane. Every day he learned more and more, but still he wasn't satisfied. Today he was thirsting for even greater knowledge.

He stood up with closed eyes, seeing the sun's red glow through his eyelids.

"Surya, I want to know you more. I know you have many of the answers that I need. I think I can never find my *Dharma* until I know you better," Traya said. Surya remained silent.

Traya began to feel the uneasiness of desperation. He sank down to his haunches and put his head in his hands. Staring at the dull earth, watching the shadows of the sun shortening, he saw, out of the corner of his eye, the glint of a shiny stone on the ground. It was as if Surya were winking at him. Traya looked down again and saw the black glowing stone lying on the ground, surrounded by many other stones and rocks of different shapes and sizes, colours and textures. As he kept looking at the stones and rocks around him, then gazing back up at the sky, he began to see that the sun was shining on all them equally. Whether big, small, black, red or

white, each one glinted and shimmered in its own way under the rays of light. Each one was special because of how it reflected the light of the sun.

We are all like that, he thought. *The one light of the Sun shines on all of us, and we all shine back in our own way. The light on each stone looks beautiful. In fact, it is because of the many different kinds of rocks that this whole mountain looks so wonderful.*

That one special stone kept shimmering in the Sun's early glow as if to send a coded message to Traya. He did not hear a voice, but he felt a force and a presence that wanted him to pick up the shiny stone that was now the centre of his attention. Now he was sure that this would be a special day.

He brushed away the rest of the earth covering the stone and picked it up. It must have been there for many years, unnoticed among all of the other stones. He held the stone in his hand and cleaned it with his thumb. It was not just an ordinary stone, for it had markings etched into it, shaped just like the sun's rays. He waited, with his heart wide open, as his father had taught him to do.

Surya silently climbed higher in the morning sky, blazing hotter and hotter, and Traya took shelter under a lone gnarled acacia tree. He sipped some water, nibbled some fruit and settled back against the tree trunk, gazing at his unusual stone.

As in a dream, Traya saw himself sit up, somehow detached, yet feeling more connected than ever. Half awake and half asleep now, Traya knew that he had found something powerful in the Sun stone. He rubbed it with his thumb and fingers, but he did not yet know what it was. He slipped the stone into his pocket, took a deep refreshing breath, and closed his tired eyes.

Chapter 4

Greeting the Sun

Teetering on the edge of the real world and the brink of a higher realm, Traya watched himself stand up and rub the stone in his pocket. As he turned to face towards Surya, the Great Sun called to him, "Come ride in my chariot with me, young Traya."

Instantly, Traya found himself seated in the magnificent chariot next to Surya, the sun, whose golden, shimmering being spilled out from behind a beautiful ornate breastplate encrusted with diamonds, and his glistening earrings sparkled with dazzling brightness. Surya's face wore a smile of immense beauty, gentleness and compassion, and his eyes danced with kindness.

"My child, I have been waiting for this moment when we could fly together. Today, Dattatraya, your heart is ready." Surya's smiling personality was just as warm as the glow surrounding him that brings life to our small planet.

"This is amazing," Traya said, gazing with squinted eyes at Surya. He didn't want to take his gaze away from the source of such joy and happiness for a moment. In his presence, Traya felt he would melt—not from heat because mysteriously there was none, but from the love that poured

out of Surya and into Traya. He seemed to be bathing in a great presence both ancient and yet ever fresh, and he felt as though he had been in Surya's chariot for eternity.

His experience was beyond words. For a moment, he imagined describing this to his mama: it was magical, mysterious, powerful, humbling, mystical. He was lost and found in the same instant, he was overawed yet befriended. Traya felt full to bursting and as vast at the universe. For a second he knew he was part of all creation; he was the tiniest molecule and at the same time the great sun himself. Tears of pure joy came from his eyes, and music exploded in his heart and mind. Every cell tingled and danced in the light. He would never feel alone again, as long as Surya was guardian of the earth. Surya coughed, and instantly Traya forgot all these wondrous things and remembered only that he was a small boy from a normal family. But the glow inside him stayed real and bright, and that feeling of knowing he was loved unconditionally and connected to all things would never be forgotten.

"What do you do all day?" Traya asked Surya.

Surya smiled and in his passionate, commanding voice, rich with laughter and rippling with power, he answered.

"I follow my *Dharma*. I do what I was born to do," replied the Great Sun, urging his five galloping horses onward across the sky. As they spoke, Traya saw the grasslands, the herds of animals and the villages as Africa glided gracefully below them.

"But what is your *Dharma*?" asked Traya. "Is it to give light to us all?"

"Yes," said Surya, "but higher than that, my *Dharma* is to give and give and give, and never ask for anything in return. This makes me eternally happy."

Traya was captivated by Surya's words. *Surya's Dharma is selfless, just like my mother's*, he thought. *Maybe all Dharmas involve giving to others and not demanding anything in return.* He listened closely as his friend continued.

"I give light to other boys and girls in all places, make the crops grow and make people happy. I lift the waters from the oceans, but I don't keep it for myself. I carry it beneath my chariot in bags you call clouds and take it to where the water needs to be. I hear people's prayers and I warm them with my light, which acts as a reminder that they are all equal children of the one Light."

"Can I find my *Dharma*?" asked Traya. "Is it different for all of us?"

"Yes," said the Great Sun. "Everyone has a special purpose for which they were born. One of my reasons for inviting you to join me today was to help guide you to discover your purpose. It's important to find that happy place inside yourself and maintain that strength throughout life."

Below them was a beautiful thick canopy of rainforest trees with greens and browns of every hue.

"Look below," Surya said, and suddenly, with a wave of his graceful hand, the clouds burst and rain thundered down on the tops of the trees. "Isn't that a wonderful sight?"

As Traya peered over the edge of the chariot, he could see the trees waving their branches in gratitude. Each leaf smiled back with a reflection of Surya's beauty after a monsoon shower.

Traya gazed below as the land slipped away.

"Surya, stop!" he called out.

"I can't," replied Surya. "Why do you want me to? What have you seen?"

Traya pointed down as huge spirals of smoke and flames rose high, raging up from the earth and almost touching their chariot. It was a forest fire.

"Drop your cloud bags now! Mother Earth needs your help!"

Surya seemed to lose his lustre for a split second. Then he said to Traya, "Not this time, my child, because men started this fire."

Traya gripped the chariot edge and demanded, "But why would they do that to such a beautiful forest?"

"Well, yesterday, when I flew past, I saw these men wanting to turn the rainforest into farmland to make a living."

"That's silly," argued Traya. "The rainforest has already told me it contains many medicines that can help cure many diseases. It gives us clean air and oxygen for the people and animals to breathe, and so much more, Surya."

"Yes, Traya, you are right. There are a few like you in the world who are awake and can hear the forest's call. But your numbers are too small, and this is the reason Mother Earth endures so much, such as this fire. Your Mother Earth has bountiful resources, and she wants you all to use them wisely for everyone's benefit.

"What Mother Earth would love is for people to be awake enough to farm responsibly and allow her to replenish for future generations.

"Sometimes disasters happen, and it's in these moments that people wake up and appreciate what they have. Take heart, young Traya! More and more people are listening to her. Often I see them walking in the woods or over mountains, enjoying their parks and gardens. The nice thing is that they are learning to love her. Out of that love, respect and care will follow."

Traya stared at the raging fire below with a blank look as he slowly shook his head in helpless bewilderment.

"Because of your caring concern today, Traya, and because I too hate to see Mother Earth suffering so much, let's help her a little."

Surya picked up his long driving whip, swirled it around his head, and cracked it over the horses' backs. They reared and shook their silvery manes, and then there came a whooshing sound. Hundreds of smiling faces appeared in front of Traya and Surya.

"Who are you?" asked Traya.

"We are Vayu—the wind," they all replied together. "At your command, Lord Surya."

"Thank you, my friends. Please, can you take these cloud bags back to that forest fire and burst them to help Mother Earth?"

"No problem!" Vayu Wind smiled and instantly grabbed bundles of cloud bags and raced back to the fire.

"Do they live in your horses' manes?" asked Traya, mesmerised by the thousands of tiny hands scooping up cloud bags and disappearing behind them.

"No," said Surya, "they are free to go anywhere, but they prefer to stay with me. There is always so much to see and do when they are with me, and my warmth gives them speed and purpose so they can accomplish their *Dharma*."

"I see," said Traya, nodding his head in understanding, "but are they always so happy?"

"Oh, yes," Surya replied, nodding vigourously. .

"Are they happy because they like giving? Is their *Dharma* the same as yours?"

"No, Traya. Vayu Wind's *Dharma* is to be free of everything. They have no possessions, no attachments and no desires. That is real freedom."

"Still, it seems that they use their freedom to give back to Mother Earth and all of her creatures and vegetation," Traya observed.

Surya smiled. He felt pride in young Traya's mature outlook.

"So if I got rid of my bed and gave away my shoes, would I be free?" Traya wondered.

"In a way," said Surya, "but being free is more of an attitude grownups need to practice. You already are very free in many ways. Having a bed is not the problem, but if someone took it away or needed it more, would you still be as happy?"

"Well, I guess so. I'd just sleep on the floor like I do when my Granny comes and sleeps in my bed."

"That's it," said Surya. "Just be happy, with a bed or without it, and be free like our wind friends. Then you can travel the earth as they do."

"That sounds like great fun," said Traya, "and easy, too."

"It is," said Surya with a twinkle in his eye. "It takes practice to be free like the Vayu Wind, but nothing you can't handle. In fact, the younger you start, the easier it is."

Chapter 5

Yamuna the River

"Do you have any children?" asked Traya, beginning to thoroughly enjoy his new adventure.

"Well, I have a daughter," Surya said proudly. He seemed to beam even more brightly for a moment. "Look, there's my daughter now! I call her Yamuna River. She loves the whole earth so much, she decided she had to travel and keep flowing. Her *Dharma*, before you ask," laughed Surya, "is to purify. Simply by thinking of her, your worries will be soothed, and wounds will be washed and salved. But she can have a temper at times too! Beware of her rocks and white water, Traya."

Traya was mesmerised by the sight of the river. Everywhere he looked, he saw silver strands of water rushing from the mountains to the sea, from lake to lake, through the thickest forests and into the farmlands. He could hear the praises from the plants and trees as they soaked up the sparkling clear liquid of life. He could feel the crops growing from the life-giving waters, and the forest animals thanked Yamuna River with every lap of their thirsty tongues. Everything was in balance and thriving. He watched, too, as the people filled their buckets and pots, taking for granted the gift that the rest of nature's flora and fauna enjoyed.

"But you know, Traya," Surya beamed like any proud papa, "whenever she reaches the ocean or a deep resting place, she comes back up to visit me. And after a good chat and some supper, she sets off again in my cloud bags to visit another place and nourish the land, the people and all creatures, great and small. In some countries, they recognise her power and harness her for electricity. Others know her spiritual power and collect her blessings as she washes away their burdens. Some simply use her goodness for their crops, and some for a pleasant swim. She doesn't mind what you do, but sometimes she does wish you would thank her a little more often. Even if you are taking a wash, you can whisper to her in your heart and she will hear you. That's the only way she can know for sure if she is fulfilling her *Dharma*."

Yamuna River looked up at the unlikely pair galloping overhead. With a wink, she disappeared under the ground, then burst out of a hole only to dive over a huge cliff.

"Look over here, Papa!" she called, and catching his rays, painted rainbows in the air.

"That's magical!" Traya exclaimed, as his eyes and smile grew wide.

"Yes," Surya replied. "She learned while sitting on my knee, watching me paint my sunrises and sunsets."

"I'm off to see my cousin Varuna. He is the vast ocean. Why don't you join us?" she called up.

"Yes, we will," said Surya. And holding his golden hand out to Yamuna River, they danced and sang down to the sea.

Varuna, the great ocean, roared and raged. Traya felt quite nervous, even though he was safe in the red and orange trimmed seats…or were they yellow and purple? The more he looked at them, the more he realised the seats seemed to be alive. They created their own kaleidoscopic collage of ever-changing colours minute by minute.

"Err. Hi," he said to Varuna the ocean, building up the courage to speak, but he could not hear a reply. "Can't he hear me?" asked Traya, a little upset because until now everyone had talked back to him.

"Yes, but you can't hear him. Varuna speaks from a very deep place and, unless you match his depth, you will never know him." Surya leaned over and whispered something to the Ocean, who began to calm down and become like a deep blue mirror with pockets of light flashing from the surface.

"Bravo!" Surya called, clapping his hands.

"What's he doing now?" Traya asked.

"It's his favourite game," said Surya. "He likes to pretend he's me and tries to shine as brightly as I do. Then he tries to copy the sky. See how blue he is? The ocean is a great master of living, Traya. Look how he stays the same when my Yamuna River rushes to embrace him, and below his surface waves, there is a still and quiet place. You can learn from him, Traya. Whatever life throws at you when you get older, remember the ocean and stay calm and still inside."

"Thank you for your wonderful message, Varuna," said Traya. " I'll come back and visit you again."

"Yes, please," lapped the waves. This time, Traya thought he could hear the words rippling through his pores and into his heart. Traya stretched and his eyelids grew heavy as he struggled to stay alert.

"Why don't you take a rest, Traya?" suggested Surya. "Here, lie back on the seats," and he gently patted the ever-changing velvet covers.

"Mmm, thanks," yawned Traya. "Just a short nap and I'll be fine."

He nestled into the cushions and seemed to melt down into nothingness. Looking up through half-closed eyes, he saw Surya settle down in his radiant armchair and begin to hum to himself. Mysterious flame-like hands began massaging Surya's shoulders as he pulled out his easel and paint brushes.

"I think we'll go for something dramatic," he said to himself. He mixed bright red with gold specks and bubbly pink and swept it across the canvas a few times.

"That the most beautiful painting I've ever seen," a weary-eyed Traya uttered incredulously from the couch.

"Thank you," said Surya, "and what's more, you'll never see another one like it. That's one of my specialties. Each one is different, always fresh and new."

He picked up the picture and gently dropped it over the side of the chariot and, then he pulled out a new canvas and chewed the end of his favourite brush, gazing with a faraway look in his eyes as if listening to someone.

"Ah, yes, a request for a romantic evening," he said and lifted his brushes, ready for a sweep of perfection from the master's hand as Traya closed his eyes.

Chapter 6

Stardust Symphony

Traya didn't know how long he slept, but a soft tinkling sound slowly came into his mind. It appeared to be simultaneously inside him and out, and it filled his body with sparkling energys.

"What's that sound?" he asked Surya. As he turned over, he saw the sun dropping an exquisite sunrise over the back of the seat.

"That's the stardust symphony, Traya. Each star has its own tune, which plays for only one soul, and because you are with me, you can hear many stars playing music together."

"Which is my star?" asked the curious boy.

"Yours is Dhruvam, the North Star, and he will be there to guide you all of your life. He will guide you when you are lost, and his song will call you home when you leave this mortal body. You only have to gaze up at night and see the sparkle, then listen with your inner ear. All will be revealed to you: the past, the present and the future. When each child is born, the stars celebrate together and, when astrologers think they are reading your future, what is really happening is that they are intuitively hearing the song of your soul."

Surya put his hand on Traya's head and then on his shoulder.

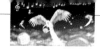

"Your time with me is getting shorter. There are two more of my friends I want you to meet."

"Do I have to go?" Traya asked with a quiver on his lips. "It's so magical being here with you, Surya. I want to stay here with you forever."

"The world needs you, Traya. This is my *Dharma*, and you must live yours. Anyway, your mum will be making your dinner soon."

"Well, I am getting hungry. I guess I can always talk to you from down below," said Traya.

Suddenly a huge plate of his favourite fruits appeared beside him on the seat.

"Help yourself, young man. I picked them for you myself."

Traya chose a huge ripe mango and cut it into two pieces with Surya's gem-studded penknife, offering one to Surya.

"No, all for you," said Surya.

"But don't you eat food?"

"No," laughed the Great Sun.

"Well, where do you get your energy from? How have you survived all these millions of years?"

"Ah, Traya, this is one of my greatest secrets. However, I will hide nothing from you. I live on the cosmic sound of infinity. I was born out of the heart of the Lord of all the Universes. I am therefore both part of Him and yet separate, and His heartbeat feeds me. It also feeds you, but you just don't know that yet. What you do know is that you are nourished by absorbing my light."

"But I thought you said I could only hear my star," interrupted Traya, who wasn't sure if he wanted to live on light and stardust, or more to the point, live without his mother's hot chapattis and chai.

"You hear only one star when you live for yourself, Traya, but when you become selfless and begin to serve others, you will hear their stars playing for you. I hear all the stars playing because I live to serve all beings equally."

"You're quite something, Surya," Traya said. "I hope one day I will come back and listen to the symphony of the stars."

"I hope you do too, my friend," said Surya and placed his hand on Traya's head. "In fact, I know you will."

The voices, prayers and petitions of millions of people were getting louder and stronger as Surya's chariot approached the dawn of a new day across the Great Ocean, and he knew his time with Traya was growing short.

"But we digress," Surya said. "I want you to look around and tell me what you can see."

Traya turned a full 360 degrees. "Not a lot," he said, "apart from your beautiful golden horses."

"What colour surrounds us?"

"Well, it's mostly blue, and high up between the stars it's nearly black."

"And what is blue, Traya?"

"The sky," shouted Traya. "Of course, I'd forgotten the sky because we are in it."

"Top marks. Now what is so special about the sky?"

"Well, it's where your cloud bags hang, where the birds fly and where you live."

"It's full of people's dreams and prayers and thoughts," added Surya. "It's the place where 'Divine Grace' descends down to earth and mixes with the prayers and longings of everyone's hearts. In the sky, angels fly, and trees transmit their messages to one another across the planet.

"It seems to separate you from the stars, but really there is no separation, Traya. You and the Infinite are one. Remember that, when we part. I will reach down to you through the sky, and you will look up to me, and one day you will stop reaching, because you will find me inside of you. My light is within you already. Remember that, Traya. Nothing separates us. We are the same even though we have different forms. Whenever the cloud bags fill the sky and I am not seen, know that, beyond all doubt, I am still there."

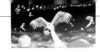

Traya felt both immensely joyful and yet saddened as he knew his adventure was coming to an end.

"How am I to get back?" he asked, feeling sure something special would happen.

"An old friend will give you a ride," Surya said and pointed behind the chariot. "Look! Here he comes."

Traya turned, and there, gaining in size as he rose into the sky, was the beautiful majestic moon. From its centre, a silver figure appeared and beckoned to Traya.

"He's my brother," said Surya, "and he lives to reflect my light to you at night. Together we are like the two eyes of the Lord, seeing and giving light to all. His name is Chandra, and he will give you a lift home on his moonbeams."

Traya turned back to Surya, and with a great smile, jumped into his strong arms to hug him.

"Thank you, Surya. You have given me so much wisdom and adventure. I promise to stay in touch with you every day."

Surya held the boy close to his chest and breathed into his hair. In that moment, Traya knew that whatever would happen in the future, he'd always have a loving friend who would look after him and care for him. That was a priceless gift.

Chapter 7

Chandra the Moon

Chandra, the moon, held out his silver arm and a pathway appeared between him and Surya.

"Come," he said, and Traya began to walk on the moonbeam towards the smiling Moon, carefully at first in case he slipped.

"Don't worry," said Chandra. "I'll hold you."

Traya turned to wave goodbye to his radiant friend as the chariot flew off into the distance. Surya's arm was raised in salute until all Traya could see was a blaze of fire and light.

Around him darkness fell and the stars twinkled.

"Destination home?" asked Chandra, in his deep, calming, almost hypnotic voice.

"Yes, please," said Traya and turned to face the smiling figure holding him in a soft haze of a nearly white light.

"Did you enjoy your ride?"

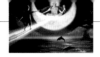

"Very much," Iraya answered.

"Well, sometime you should come and join me again when we can spend more time together."

"I'd like that," Traya said, and then he got a curious look on his face.

"What is it?" asked the Moon, putting his hand on Traya's shoulder.

"Chandra, what is your *Dharma*? Surya's light is vibrant and yours seems gentler. Still, you both light the sky, but in different ways."

Chandra smiled and drew Traya closer to him. Soothing Traya with his ancient presence, he began to explain.

"I have been reflecting Surya's light for millions of years, and my *Dharma* is to shine brightly at the other end of the day. I try to remain humble and grateful because, without him, I am simply a mass of rock floating in a vast galaxy, an empty planet. He gives me purpose. I shine because he shines on me. My light is his, and it is my great honour to pass on some of his rays through the night sky. I am strong too, Traya. Never think that the quiet ones are weak!"

Traya looked up at Chandra's silver eyes and felt he was falling into some deep and ancient mystery. "Tell me about your powers, please," asked Traya, wanting to know the secrets of this enigmatic nighttime character.

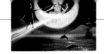

Chandra beamed at his eager new student.

"Well, I play many roles, not unlike your mother."

Traya thought about his mother's many roles as mother, wife, and teacher.

"One of my main powers is to light the night sky, of course, and to help people see their way through the darkness. I am mostly known for my control of the oceans on the earth, like Varuna, whom you have just met. The tides rise and fall to my call, as I wax and wane through monthly and yearly rhythms. The wise farmers and gardeners use my lunar timetable for the correct time to plant the crops and harvest the fields. There is much to be learned about this as Mother Earth and all her creatures depend on cycles of time.

"Your mother is a wise woman, and she knows to cut your hair only when she sees me growing in the sky. This means you will not lose energy, as your hair is an extension of your nervous system. The native people, like the American Indians, know this. They would keep their hair long and their men would avoid shaving. Little things like this matter to me, but are often lost in the rush of modern life.

"I also affect people's minds and emotions, especially at full moon, and those sensitive to my rays may struggle a bit, but I mean no harm. They just need a little help to stay balanced. The women of the world all know my power to influence the cycles of their body and the gift

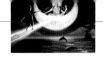

of childbirth. However, little one, your mother and father will teach you much of this when you are older."

They rode the moonbeams in silence for a long, beautiful moment. Traya looked down and saw the ocean's waves following Chandra's powerful attraction.

"I'm not sure if I want to meet the Ocean again, Chandra. He was a bit scary."

"Varuna the Ocean is not so bad," said Chandra. "You just have to know how to handle him, as I do. He seems so huge and unwieldy, but he readily obeys my call. I can teach you how to understand him."

"Thanks," said Traya, "but not for a while." Traya was deeply moved by the sheer power of Chandra's silent work, and how he humbly added to everyone's life without them ever knowing.

Traya stifled a yawn, and his eyelids started to flutter as he struggled to stay awake.

"Here, lie down on my bed and, when we arrive in the sky near your house, you can slide safely down my moonbeam to the spot where Surya picked you up in his chariot."

Traya lay back in a gossamer fine hammock and swung between two stars as he gazed back into Chandra's serene face. He curled his legs up and asked softly, "Why do you wax and wane? Why don't you stay the same like Surya?"

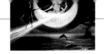

"That's a good question and one that few ask," said Chandra, "because they fear the truth of my answer. I do this to show you that your life, too, is made up of phases. You start as a baby, and then grow in power into childhood, then teenage years, and adulthood. And, as old age comes, you lose your strength and, finally, your spirit leaves your body and your life on earth comes to an end. Each time, I feel the excitement and possibilities while I grow and the somber sadness and loss when I diminish. But I always come back again. I'm trying to show you that, whatever happens to your body, your soul remains immortal and indestructible. You are greater than your body, Traya, and, remember, you are also a spark of the infinite universe."

"But why are people afraid of knowing that they are part of the infinite universe?" questioned Traya, thinking it was very reassuring to know there was no end.

Chandra smiled to himself. "Traya, fear holds everyone back from finding themselves because they know that when they do, enormous power will surge through their beings, and with that power you can do great things.

"When you know yourself, you will feel your interconnection with all of life and, in that moment, selfish thoughts and desires end. Then you will live for the benefit of others, like my brother, Surya. It is the ultimate destination for everyone, but few understand this secret and even fewer have the courage to find this power and freedom."

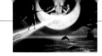

"But you did," commented Traya.

"Yes, and now I try to pass on that secret to those who meditate with me in the night or the small hours of the early morning." Chandra smiled again.

"Everyone I've met who gives to others is very, very happy," said Traya thoughtfully, beginning to feel he was getting into things he could not yet understand.

"Let me simplify this a bit," Chandra offered. "Happiness is our true nature. When you live true to yourself and others, it will blossom inside of you."

Traya had closed his eyes and was swinging in the hammock with a wonderful feeling of contentment seeping through his consciousness. He could practise being happy and, just for a split second, he thought he could understand what Chandra was saying. Lying there cosy and relaxed, he was drifting away, far into the distance. Suddenly he awoke with a start.

"Chandra!" he called out.

Far up in the sky, he saw the full moon hanging in front of a glimmering curtain of stars. Traya was lying in a pool of silken moonlight under the acacia tree. He couldn't see the hammock, but all around him on the ground were spider webs glistening in the soft evening light.

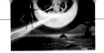

"Thank you so much!" he called out, and his tummy rumbled in agreement. He felt the stone in his pocket, leaped to his feet and, with the moonlight illuminating his path, ran all the way back to his house on the edge of the plains.

What a wonderful adventure I've had, he thought. *Mama and Papa will be really excited when I tell them.* But now, as his feet flew over the rough path, he was thinking only about the supper that would be waiting for him beside the fire.

Chapter 8

Papilio the Butterfly

When Traya awoke the next morning, he lay in bed for a moment. Watching the play of sunlight across his threadbare blanket, he wondered:

Was yesterday's journeying a dream, or did I really visit Surya and his family and friends? It must have been real, Otherwise how else would I have learned so much?

He reached out and caught a beam of light with his hand and whispered, "I love you, Surya. Please play with me again today."

Just then, an exquisite butterfly gently fluttered out of a dark corner and began to dance in the light above his hand.

"I'm here to play with you," said Papilio, the butterfly, in a sweet, girlie voice. She landed on his outstretched finger, showing off her pretty wings.

"Your markings are really beautiful," said Traya, and she quivered with excitement at the compliment. "Did Surya paint them for you?"

"No, the Little People in the forest do it for me."

"Which people?" asked Traya, wondering why he hadn't seen any people painting butterflies on his recent walks.

"The ones who live in the trees. You probably can't see them because you don't believe they exist," said Papilio, and danced a jig to show off her dazzling colours. "That is the main thing you have to remember. What you want to see will be shown to you."

"Try that one again?" said Traya, scrunching his eyebrows in confusion. "It's too early for riddles."

"It's simple," fluttered Papilio. "If you want to see beauty everywhere, you will. If you think an ordinary thing like a tree is just a piece of wood and not a living thing, that's all you will see. If you want to see magical things, all you have to do is look for them and they will appear to you."

"You mean like Unicorns and Little People?" asked Traya, getting very interested now, "and angels and the Vayu Wind?"

"Yes! Exactly!" said his little friend, who now began to dance on Traya's head.

"Well, that's what we will do today!" said Traya, and he waved his hand around as if to capture his new friend. "Do you want to come and play with me this morning?"

"Yes!" said his new friend, Papilio. She landed on his shoulder and stroked his cheek gently with her wings. "We can go to the forest and look for the Little People."

After breakfast, they set off along the trail to the forest together, with zebras grazing in the distance and a few tall giraffes nibbling the green leaves on the tops of the trees. The early morning light was burning off the dew on the grass. The day ahead brimmed with adventure yet to be discovered.

"This way," said Papilio, and they headed into a wooded valley where a happily laughing river followed the path.

"Hi, Yamuna River! You seem to be having fun today," called Traya.

She rippled back a swift greeting, "Hello! Gotta go!"

The path started to get smaller and smaller, and Traya began to get a little worried.

"I'm not sure we should be here," he said. "There are lots of wild animals and poisonous snakes. Maybe we should turn back."

Just as he said that, Traya slipped. The earth seemed to crumble away beneath his feet. He felt himself sliding down a muddy bank. His arms waved wildly, trying to find something to grab

hold of. After a few seconds, he stopped falling and, landing with a jolt, rolled over a few times. The air felt musty and cool, and the light was much dimmer at the bottom of this hole.

"Ouch!" he said out loud, feeling sore and a bit stunned, but mostly feeling foolish.

"You've got me into trouble now!" said Traya, as he imagined what his parents would think when they found his bones down in this hole at some future date. His skin crawled, and he shivered as fear loomed large in his mind. "I've fallen into some kind of trap."

"Don't worry! We'll find a way out," said his friend. "I'll go for help." Papilio flew up into the air and caught a warm draft that carried her towards the sun, showing off her beautiful kaleidoscope of colours.

Traya's heart pounded as he looked around at the dark, muddy walls rising another four feet above his head. He tried to climb out, but the moist dirt would not support him. The walls simply crumbled at his touch, and his feet sank down into the cloying earth below. He suddenly felt very afraid. No one knew where he was, and a night in the wilderness was too dangerous to think about. No amount of talking to a hungry pride of lions, or a greedy pack of hyenas, would change their mind. He would be their supper! Time passed, and he felt hot and dirty and more and more scared, but Traya was not one to panic easily. He raised his eyes to the sky and called to Surya.

"Please help me! I'm stuck."

"It's okay, Traya. Every situation creates a chance to meet someone or learn something new. And, remember, I promised to look after you."

It was real, Traya thought. *Surya has never answered me so quickly and clearly before. Now we are true friends after my ride in his chariot.*

Traya felt happier and more confident after Surya's reassurance, and settled down quietly to wait for help.

Chapter 9

Pythagoras the Python

Traya didn't have to wait long. Soon, he heard a slithering noise over the edge of the pit.

"Who's there?" he called out, and down flew Papilio.

"Help is here!" she cried, fluttering her designer wings.

Traya wasn't too sure he liked the sound he could hear in the undergrowth.

"It's my friend, Pythagoras."

As if on cue, a long head, neck and body glided gracefully down the hole and hung over Traya's head.

"Hellooo!" bellowed the enormous python, as his forked tongue slithered between his sharp fangs, which glistened frighteningly in the single ray of sun that had sneaked between the leaves and branches. "My name is Pythagoras, Py to my friends," he introduced himself in his booming but oddly comforting voice.

Traya's mind told him to be frightened, but his instinct told him everything was okay. Surya's warm smile, the introduction from his beautiful winged friend and the reassuring calmness of nature all around him calmed him despite the looming presence of this huge serpent.

"Pleased to meet you, Py. I'm Traya."

"In a spot of bother, I see," said Py with a grin, swaying over Traya's head like a pendulum.

"Yeah! I'm stuck," said Traya with a grimace.

"Quite so, quite so. Well, not to worry. I'll pull you out in a jiffy. Let me spin around," Py said as he coiled around a tree branch high above them, "and I'll give you my tail."

He lowered his strong tail down to Traya and wrapped it around his chest. Traya shivered a little at the thought of being wrapped in the coils of a python. This was not his idea of a rescue!

"He needs a little more of your tail, Py," said his fluttering friend as she slid down two meters of warm, dry, thick coils.

The tail curled round and poked Traya in the ribs. "Ouch!" said Traya, and before he knew it, he was wrapped in a vice-like grip.

"Go ahead and lift him out," said Papilio, floating gracefully around them both. Slowly Py pulled Traya up. He felt the suction of the wet earth release his feet, and the long, strong creature pulled him safely up and out of the hole. Py put him gently down on a bed of leaves away from the pit and released his hold.

"Thank you, Py," said Traya, a little out of breath from Py's tight squeeze. "You're a star. What can I give you in return?"

"Not a thing, young Tray. There is nothing I need in particular," Py said humbly. "It was no effort for me at all. I'm a python. Coiling and lifting is what I do. Besides, I like to live a simple life. I eat food when it comes my way, and I fast when it doesn't. I accept life as it is in that moment. That's my purpose. And that makes me happy."

"Well," said Traya, "in that case, Py, you must come home with me for some nice, fresh milk."

"Well, now, that sounds quite delicious actually. Thank you, young man. I accept!" Py dropped down from the branch, brushing past Traya's shoulders for a moment and rubbing his neck fondly with his rough skin.

"Do you live alone, Py?" Traya asked as they weaved their way along the forest trail with Papilio flitting playfully above.

"Yes," said Py, "I find it easier. Most snakes find seclusion preferable."

"Why?" asked Traya. "I like having friends around me."

"But, do you really?" asked Py, with a slightly airy hiss returning to his speech.

"Well, I guess I prefer those friends who understand me and who like animals and nature as I do."

"That's my angle," replied Py with a grin. "Here, in the wilds, we find our peace with ourselves, and avoid those who don't understand us. You should be careful too, Traya. Watch whom you spend time with, and always choose friends who will keep you safe."

Suddenly, Py turned his head quickly to his right. "Danger!" hissed Py. "Quick, follow me." Like an army officer, Py was in command. He quickly slipped off the path and vanished into the bushes.

Traya obediently squirmed after him, groaning as the thorns caught his arms and legs.

"Climb up here," hissed Py. He watched as Traya followed him up a gnarled tree. "Hide in the creepers," he whispered, already invisible in the greenery.

"What's wrong?" whispered Traya, nervously looking out between the leaves.

"It's the hunter," Py said, with a nervous but fierce look in his eye. "Look over there by the river."

Traya peered out and saw a tall man wearing camouflage clothing and carrying a large rifle. He was poised, preparing to shoot.

"He's seen a deer drinking by the river, but we are all game to him. See his concentration and single pointed gaze? That's what makes him dangerous," Py explained, nudging Traya's head back into the foliage.

"I have nothing to fear from him," said Traya, "because I am not game to him. But now I understand. The danger you feel from the hunter is the same fear of imminent doom I get from the lions and, well, some of the other snakes in the jungle."

"Shhhh," Py hissed.

Traya nodded. *I hope he doesn't hit the deer. I love them. They are such beautiful creatures, so gentle and kind.*

Just as he sent out this thought, the hunter lifted his hand and swatted at something above his head. The deer caught the movement and bolted into the forest.

"Look! He's safe." Traya wriggled with excitement.

"Be ssstill," hissed Py, as his serpentine instincts began to overtake his more civilised nature. "We are ssstill in danger. You may be sssafe, but you can bring danger to me."

Py wrapped himself around the boy to hold him still. Traya knew he had no chance of escape from Py's strong embrace, so he accepted his situation and relaxed into the python's firm but comfortable coils.

"Do you think I could have that concentration?" whispered Traya almost inaudibly into Py's ear next to his head.

"Just read my mind," Py transmitted to his friend silently, "and I'll read yours. Of course you can concentrate like that. You just need to practise meditation. Remember, your mind is like an arrow. Whatever target you set for yourself, that is what you will hit."

The hunter disappeared out of human earshot, and Py began to speak out loud again. "Do me a favour will you, Traya?" murmured Py, now peering at him straight in the eyes.

"Sure," said Traya, transfixed by the Python's mesmerising gaze.

"Always choose a worthy, compassionate target, like being happy and free. Never let your arrow-like mind loose on negative things."

"Yesss," Traya hissed back obediently to those commanding, unblinking eyes.

"You don't mind if I disturb your little *tête-á-tête* do you?" asked Papilio, dancing happily as she returned to her friends, breaking their gaze. "Did you see me!" she boasted, fluttering her wings enthusiastically. "Wasn't I brave and fast?"

"What? Wh…where…" stuttered Traya, shaking his head as if coming out of a trance.

"The hunter, silly! While you two were hiding and sitting around, I decided to help the deer."

"Oh! It was you buzzing around the hunter's head!" Traya exclaimed. "Well done, little friend, but it was a dangerous thing to do. You could have been swatted down."

"See," she said, "we all have our uses."

"Brilliant move," said Py, ever the strategic soldier as he released his hold on Traya. "Even the smallest actions can make a big difference. With just your little wings, you accomplished something that even I could not. Come on. It's lunchtime!" He dropped out of the tree with a light thud. "The deer had a lucky escape today, chaps," said Py, his polished professional voice returning, and his eyes looking more human than snakelike again. "But we still need to be careful here in the forest."

Chapter 10

The Little People

"Why didn't the deer see the hunter?" Traya asked as they walked, flew, and slithered along. "They are usually very careful."

"It was the sound of the river," Py answered. "He was so absorbed in listening to the beautiful song of Yamuna River that he forgot to stay alert."

"It's okay to enjoy the beauties of life, but not to be lost in them," added Papilio, alighting on a beautiful orchid and sipping its nectar.

"Take a fish," said Py, warming to the subject. "There it is, swimming around free as the river and, suddenly, it sees a big juicy worm. Instead of thinking, *Why is that land worm hanging unmoving in my river?* Gulp, it's swallowed, and so is his freedom and probably his life."

"But I like my food," said Traya.

"Why, we all do, of course, young man," rippled Py as he negotiated a wide, black line of army ants on the path. "But the point is: does it like you more? Are you in control of what you eat or does the desire for food consume you?"

Traya laughed and thought back to the time when he was smaller and had taken a pocketful of sweets to his bed. Halfway through the night, he awoke to find he was sharing his mattress with a family of mice that were eating the remainder of his sweets.

Traya suddenly felt that something was wrong and a shiver ran up his spine.

Where's Papilio? he thought and spun around.

Py was chattering on and had disappeared around the corner.

"Help me!" the butterfly squeaked in a frightened voice.

Traya peered under a branch, and there was his beautiful friend—caught in a huge spider web.

"Get me out of here quick!" she said urgently, and wriggled a little more, getting even more tangled up in the web.

"Don't move, Papilio, or you might hurt yourself or tear your wings," Traya ordered. He checked to see if the spider was around. He knew that some spiders have a deadly bite. Then, he carefully removed the fine threads around Papilio and pulled her free.

He walked up the path a bit before sitting down on a large rock and gently teased away the threads from Papilio's wings, being careful not to hurt her. Meanwhile, Py had rushed back to find them both.

He had watched Traya free his friend from the spider's trap and couldn't help but say, "There you are! That's just my point. If she hadn't gone to sip nectar from that rare flower, she would not have been caught in the web."

"Give her a break," said Traya. "She nearly died. Here, let her rest on your back for a bit and I'll bring her a flower to drink from."

Just as he said that, a tiny being appeared by his side carrying a ruby red teacup.

"Here, drink, Papilio. It's a healing herbal nectar." The little man's voice was sharp and shrill, almost like the wings of a mosquito.

"This is my friend. He's one of the Little People," said Papilio, gulping down the powerful juice.

"Pleased to meet you, Traya," said the tiny figure, dressed in delicate petal-like clothes. "Your kindness is known to all of us. All your actions are noticed and, in return, we try to fill your life with miracles."

"Oh...you know who I am!" said Traya, quite surprised and a bit embarrassed by the compliment. Then he realized what the man had said. "What kind of miracles?"

"Well, let's see, like sending you our emissary, Papilio, to play with you; inviting you to travel with Surya, and giving you the sun stone to help you remember him; guiding you to find your pet deer last year.

"We, the Little People, have the privilege of being the eyes, ears and voice of Mother Earth. That's our *Dharma*. We communicate her wishes to all the other beings, and we want you to know that she will always support you, feed you and give you shelter."

"Wow. You really have been watching over me. Thank you," Traya said, and bowed low to the little man, who looked almost translucent.

"Must go now," the man said, disappearing into a patch of light between two ferns. "Work to do! More wings to paint!" And he was gone just as quickly as he had arrived.

"They know everything," said Papilio, perking up and feeling much better after her tonic.

"You can ride back on my shoulder," said Traya. "I'm getting hungry now." With purpose in his stride, he turned back along the path towards his home and family.

"Spiders can be dangerous critters," said Papilio, "but marvellous as well." She was now feeling quite cheerful and warming her wings in the sun. "They make their webs and can remove them again in a day. Quite fascinating! The Little People say they are very spiritual beings," she added.

"Why's that?" asked Traya, thinking of both their beautiful gossamer webs and their dangerous bite.

"Well," Papilio continued, "according to the little folk, who instruct us in the natural laws while they paint our wings, spiders know that nothing is permanent. The silky fibres of their webs are stronger than steel, yet almost invisible to the eye. They are a symbol of the fine line between this physical world and the spiritual world into which all of us are invited, but few choose to enter. They understand how real both worlds are. Their minuscule threads come from inside of them and can build a magnificent web. This reminds each one of us that we have an immense creative potential ready to be pulled out of our hearts and minds and given to the world."

"Their webs are beautiful, aren't they?" Traya added, stepping over Py, who had gone to investigate a rustling sound in the roadside.

"And, as I said earlier, nothing in this physical world stays the same. Change is inevitable. They build a glorious gossamer home and, with the stroke of a hand, it's gone."

Traya shuffled his feet in the dirt. "I guess I should have apologised after wrecking the web."

"Well, do it now!" said Papilio excitedly.

"I can't," Traya said. "We are too far away from the spider. He won't hear me."

"The Little People will," Papilio replied. "They hear all your prayers and heartfelt thoughts, and Surya does too. They will pass on the message."

"Okay. I'll try." Traya closed his eyes and imagined the spider and its web far away. "I'm sorry I broke your web, Mr Spider. Please forgive me."

Traya looked around and put his ear to the sky, waiting for some kind of sign or response. "See, nothing happened," said Traya.

"Yes, it did!" Papilio exclaimed. "Look!"

From nowhere a gust of wind arose, bringing with it a flurry of fallen blossoms from a nearby tree. One flower landed at his feet.

"Ah! I see how it works," Traya said excitedly, with a little dance in his step as he leapt into the pile of petals. He was happy to know he could send his thoughts and prayers from a distance, knowing they would be heard.

Chapter 11

Spinning Honey

While eating lunch back home, Traya introduced his friend, Py, to his mother, who went into the kitchen carrying a large bowl of milk for him.

"This is a real treat," said Py. "Please thank your mother for me."

"He can have the main roof beam to sleep around," said Ana, quite used to accommodating Traya's strange friends. "He might even find some of his friends and relatives up there.

"Pythons are useful for keeping the rats away," she said to Traya. "I'm sure he will find something more substantial when he's hungry."

After partaking of their simple meal, they all retired to rest for a while, as Surya was at his highest and it was too hot to run and play outside. Papilio took the bedpost, Py curled around the rafters of the roof and Traya lay under his mosquito net on the old bed. After a morning filled with adventure, he was soon fast asleep.

Surya was cooling off behind some wispy white clouds when Traya awoke nearly an hour later and gave his face a quick wash. Py decided to rest for a while longer, so Traya and Papilio went in search of some lemonade and sat in the garden.

Ana had been waiting for Traya to wake up, as she needed some honey from the Beekeeper who lived by the water lily ponds. She gave him a few coins and an empty pot, and Traya was only too delighted to go off honey shopping. The lily ponds were very special, and often he would see hippos playing with their young in the deep water, eagles soaring overhead and lions coming for a cool drink.

He would be safe with the Beekeeper, who lived overlooking the ponds in a house on stilts. The Beekeeper was a wise and wrinkled old man who kept many hives and had the sweetest honey. The bees were happy, as there was an abundance of flowers near the ponds and lots of sunshine. When they arrived, they found the Beekeeper spinning the honey from the combs.

"Can I help?" asked Traya.

"Sure," said the Beekeeper. "Stand here and turn this handle. Inside the drum is the honeycomb, and we spin it around very fast to bring out the honey."

The honey was dripping out of the drum and into big pots at his feet, and Traya kept turning the handle until the sweat poured from his brow.

"Take a rest, young man," said the kind old man. "Sit here and have some honey wax to suck."

"It's delicious," said Traya a short time later, his face smeared in golden honey. Even Papilio was taking a sip from the droplets that had fallen onto Traya's knees.

Traya thought, *This is heavenly*, as he chewed honey wax and looked out over the lily ponds. Surya was painting a beautiful red sky; herds of antelope were coming down to the watering hole; and a pot full of beeswax was just waiting to be sucked. He politely spat the wax into his hand after all the honey was sucked away and threw it in the rubbish box.

"Why do you like bees so much?" he asked his old friend, who was busy cutting the wax top off another honeycomb and placing it in the spinning drum.

"Now, then," said the beekeeper thoughtfully, while pausing to wipe his knife on a bunch of leaves, "I suppose it's because they are so gentle and generous. They sip only a little nectar from each flower and leave lots for other creatures to drink, and they make enough honey to share with all of us. That's it!" he said, going back to the precision task of taking only a very fine layer of wax from the honeycomb surface. He always took extra time and care to make sure he didn't waste any honey or damage the combs. Later he would return the wooden frame with the now empty honey combs back into the hives so the bees could use them again. It helped the bees not to have to start from scratch to make the wax combs. Nothing was wasted from the bees, as the wax capping would be used for candles and sold as polish.

"There would be no hunger in our world, Traya, if mankind lived like the bees. We would only take from the earth what we really needed and leave the rest for others. There would be no waste or overconsumption. Also," he added, handing Traya another slice of wax to suck, "if we shared our riches with others, no one would go without. The same principle applies to our interactions with people," he said. "You see, if we only invited the best qualities from each other, and gave of our sweetest talents, the world would be a very happy place."

Traya nodded. He was beginning to understand the *Dharma* of the bees and the important lesson they had for all creatures about sharing the fragile bounty of Mother Nature.

The sun was beginning to set behind them when the old man looked up from his spinning. "I'll walk you home," he said. "It will be dark soon, and there are lions about."

He had already filled the pot for Ana, and he poured in a little extra for her because, whenever she came by, she always took the time to talk with him and help him with small tasks. And, as was the custom, Traya left the coins on the beekeeper's chair. The beekeeper never liked to take money from Traya's family, as they were poor, but Traya's parents knew the laws of giving and receiving and didn't want to be indebted to anyone. The old beekeeper, who was also far from wealthy, honoured their wishes. He, too, knew that when you receive or take something from the

abundant universe, then you are indebted to that source, and you should give something back in return. He had discovered, as a young man that, when he kept taking and taking, wanting more and more, there had come a point when it all came crashing down round his ears, and no one wanted to be around him anymore. When he took up beekeeping, the bees began to teach him about the balance between that which we take from life and that which we need to put back.

The old man, with his ebony staff in hand, walked in silence with the young boy and Papilio, savouring the night air together. Dogs barked nearby and mosquitoes buzzed past their ears, but nothing could destroy that tranquil feeling of peaceful comfort, caught between the scent of nightfall and the lighting of cooking fires in the distance.

The Beekeeper left Traya and Papilio as they turned down the track towards their house.

"Goodnight!" called Traya, but the old man had already become one with the darkness. He was a man who had made peace with himself and his world.

Traya was tired as he walked the last few meters to his house, putting one foot carefully in front of the other until he could see the faint glow of their kitchen lamp.

Traya placed the honey on the table and called out, "I'm home!"

He joined his parents in the sitting area around the fire, and his mother brought him a warm cup of milk.

"I've learned a lot today," he said with a yawn, and sat down by the fire next to his father. "You know, Papa," Traya said as he sipped his hot milk, "I go to the best school and have the best teachers in the world."

Atri's reply was a smile and a single nod. He took comfort knowing that his son was learning many of the important lessons that would make him competent, strong and sure of himself as a man. He knew that formal book learning would come when the time was right but, for now, Traya was innocent and in love with life. He was experiencing the power of Spirit in harmony with creation and was receiving a priceless gift found only through living in the present moment with passion and joy. All of the more academic lessons would make so much more sense once Traya understood himself and his world.

"I'm very proud of you, my son," Atri whispered to Traya and pulled his son's head to his chest.

"Papa," Traya said, barely able to keep his eyes open, "what's your *Dharma*?" Then he fell into a sound sleep and slumped onto his father's lap.

Atri smiled and, holding his answer for another day, carried Traya to his sleeping area and

tucked him up in bed, kissing him goodnight. Papilio floated past Py, who was still sleeping in the rafters, and then fluttered to the windowsill to take her rest there so she would get the first rays of the rising sun.

Chapter 12

Russell the Squirrel

Surya's piercing rays shot through the window like fiery arrows straight onto Traya's face.

"Arise, little warrior," Surya called. "You have much to do today."

Papilio was already up and had breakfasted from the flowers below the window, and Py had a strange lump somewhere near his middle. Traya yawned, and looked up to say good morning to Py. The python stared back with a misty look in his eyes.

"Hi," he hissed back and then burped. "Pardon me," he said, shifting the lump a little.

"What's wrong? Are you ill?" Traya exclaimed. "Have you hurt yourself?"

"No, silly, that's my dinner."

Traya looked down. "Oh," he said, not wanting to ask who or what was now inside the python.

"You don't mind if I hang out here and sleep for a week or so, do you?" Py asked, his eyes already closed.

"Not at all," said Traya, remembering that today he wanted to go and see a baby elephant and his close friend Asha, at the nearby animal sanctuary. "As long as you don't slither in your sleep and get under my mother's feet. Just stay where you are and sleep as long as you want."

He put on clean shorts and a tee shirt and had breakfast.

"Another adventure today, Traya?" asked Pipilio with a lazy yawn.

Traya laughed. "Everyday, Papilio." Traya could see that the fragile little creature was still exhausted from all their other adventures. "But would you mind staying here to keep Py company and take care of my mama for me? I know it would really make her happy to have a beautiful butterfly with her all day."

"Anything for my friend, Traya! Have a fun day!"

With an apple in his pocket and a Ganesh chant in his heart, he set off for the nearby wild animal sanctuary, where he would find the elephants.

Ganesh, his father had explained, was the elephant part of the Great Spirit. With his great strength and memory, he helped remove all the problems and challenges from everyone's lives. It was a simple chant: *Ganesha Sharanam, Sharanam Ganesha.* By chanting it, he was inviting the universal force of love to flow freely in his life. The chant became synchronised with his stride and each step became a prayer and a blessing for the earth. Traya strode out, and imagined himself stepping in rhythm with the beat of the earth.

Within the hour, he had reached the sanctuary. He looked around for the young girl who lived there. Asha was a year older and a head taller than Traya. Her mother was African and her father English. She had beautiful golden skin, long braided hair and eyes that looked deep inside you and glistened like Chandra's when she smiled. She loved to play with Traya, and she was a special friend of his. Together they always had wonderful adventures in the bush and at the sanctuary where her father was a vet.

Eventually, Traya found Asha nursing a sick squirrel and feeding it by hand. She often helped her father take care of injured and sick animals that had been taken to him for help. Traya loved to help as well.

"Hi!" he called out to her with his brightest smile. "Want a hand?"

Her eyes sparkled when she saw her friend. "Yes!" she replied. "You're just in time. You have healing hands, so you can hold little Russell. I called him that because he rustles in the branches when he runs up and down. Here, help me give him these seeds."

Traya held the frightened squirrel and sang to him. Soon he had calmed down enough to eat a little.

"What happened to you, little friend?" Traya asked, looking at the sores on its back.

"I was attacked by some big birds," Russell the Squirrel replied.

"But why?" Traya asked. "Birds don't normally attack squirrels."

"Well, I was bringing a bunch of berries home in my mouth, and they wanted to steal them. They pecked and pecked me until I let go. Then they took my berries and flew off. It was a painful but valuable lesson," Russell said.

"What lesson?" Traya asked, knowing that he could learn from every animal and every situation in life.

"Well, I have learned that sometimes it's better to be humble and let go, than to hang on and get hurt."

Traya thought about it, and decided that it made a lot of sense.

"We are simple, easy-going beings," continued the injured squirrel. "Grandpapa Squirrel

always used to tell us never to get too attached to something or someplace because, if you lost it, you would feel hurt. When I was tiny, the whole of the family used to sit together in the branches, lit up by fireflies. He would puff up his tail and point up to Chandra at night and remind us that life is like the moon, ever fresh and ever changing. I think his spirit came back to teach me as I had become a bit of a hoarder and was getting too greedy," Russell said thoughtfully, chewing some crushed seeds out of Traya's hand.

Asha rubbed her fingers through the soft fur of Russell's neck and head as he continued the conversation that only he and Traya could understand.

"Grandpapa lived by the simple old ways, and we loved to hear his stories of the past."

"What else did he say?" Traya interrupted the chatty squirrel, who could talk as fast as he could chew.

"Well, he told us of the great forests that reached across the world before mankind fell out of harmony with Mother Earth, and how our kind could travel for months in the treetops without ever touching the ground. He told us that the trees would talk to the animals and were the voice of Mother Earth, whispering her secrets to us all. Can you hear the trees whispering, Traya?" the squirrel asked, looking up into the boy's brown eyes.

"Yes, I can," said Traya. "They do seem to talk to me sometimes, especially when I put my ear to their bark and listen to the sap flowing."

The squirrel continued to look at Traya as if searching for something.

"Traya," he whispered, "I'll tell you one more secret about the trees."

Traya held his breath and waited for another of nature's secrets to be revealed.

"The trees are Mother Earth's soul doctors. They can heal any pain in your heart or wound in your mind. Sit or play amongst them like I do," urged Russell, "especially when the fireflies are out. You will become healthier and happier as you hear their healing whispers." With that he stopped talking and munching and fell into a deep restful sleep. Traya placed him gently into his box of straw and turned to Asha to tell her what had happened to the animal, and why it had been attacked.

"The same thing happened to me!" she said excitedly. "One day, I was walking along with a bag of fruit for the elephants and a pack of baboons saw me. They chased me, and I dropped the bag of fruit, which they grabbed and ran off. They didn't hurt me, but it was a bit scary," she added. "They were almost as big as me, and I learned the same lesson as Russell. Don't get too attached to things."

Together they quietly moved away, leaving the sleeping, twitching squirrel to rest and dream of never-ending forests and fireflies.

"Come on, let's visit the elephants," Asha said, putting some more food in a bowl on the floor. "They will be back now from their morning bath in the river."

Chapter 13

Meeting the Baby Elephant

They strolled together hand in hand over the hill towards the elephants' enclosure. Asha was keen to show Traya a new addition to her favourite big animals, and was almost pulling Traya along. Traya was excited to see the elephants too, and was enjoying the journey with Asha.

From the top of the rolling hill, they could see the keepers feeding the elephants with grasses, leaves and fruits, and they both broke into a run.

"Come and see the new young one we rescued after the poachers killed its mother!" Asha said excitedly as she dragged Traya over to the smallest elephant in the herd.

Traya held out his apple to the small grey creature, and in a flash, it was picked up by a deft little trunk and munched with relish. Before he knew it, Traya was being frisked all over in search of more delicious treats. He laughed as the little nose searched down his shirt and ruffled his hair. He gazed into a pair of eyes that looked both humanly present and from a time and place beyond memory.

"They love to touch and be touched," Asha said, embracing the little elephant called Timba, who nuzzled her in return. "In the wilds they are always in close physical contact with each other."

"Just like us humans," said Traya, who still liked to cuddle up beside his mother and father even though he was quite grown up.

"In our family, we massage each other's feet and shoulders," said the little girl, "especially if one of us is not feeling very well. There is a kind of healing that comes through touch."

"And a special bond of family and friendship," Traya said with a smile. He and Asha seemed to automatically link arms. They giggled as Traya helped Asha up onto the stone wall and then pulled himself up and sat next to her.

They watched in peaceful silence as the keepers began to rub down the elephants' tough hides with coconut shells.

Asha was lost in thought as she bounced her heels off the stone wall. Then she nudged Traya's foot with hers. "Wouldn't the world be a nicer place," she suggested, leaning back on her hands and looking up at the sky as she slowly inhaled the warm fresh air, "if everyone hugged each other every day the way these elephants do?"

The playful calves were rubbing their trunks along each other's backs and ears, and the watching children both felt the love and joy the elephants were bringing to the world.

Traya looked happily at his friend and nodded in wholehearted agreement.

"But, you know, some people don't understand real hugging," he said. "These animals know it and we know it too. Hugging brings so much comfort and happiness into everyone's lives. Last year I saw a lady who looked like she really needed a hug."

"What do you mean?" asked the golden-skinned girl, who had known nothing of life beyond her home on the ranch.

"Well, last year, I went with my parents to a wedding in the big city. As we were taking the bus home at night, a woman wearing a shiny dress and lots of make-up got on and she was crying."

"That sounds very strange," said Asha. "Why was she so unhappy?"

"That's what I was wondering too," said Traya. "My papa could see that I was confused. He told me that he recognised her from when he and mama had first arrived in Kenya. She had been filling every moment of her life with work to keep up appearances, not realising that time was passing her by. She seemed more concerned about herself, Papa said, than caring and sharing with the community.

"She probably had never found time for a best friend, a partner or a family, and had missed the joys of sharing, hugging and laughing together," Traya continued. "Just look at the elders in our village. They have such deep, lined faces and yet they are always laughing and surrounded by joy. How you look doesn't change what's in your heart.

"Also, Asha," Traya said, thinking of something else he had learned, "my mama is always telling me you can never find happiness in someone else until you have found it within yourself. Love and happiness don't come from the hug, but the hug is an expression of the happiness and trust that two people have already found in each other."

Asha turned towards Traya and felt the warm glow of friendship growing inside her.

"I think I know what you mean, Traya," she said softly, as she thought about the woman Traya and his father had seen on the bus. "I like you because of your love for the animals, the way you laugh so much and how you talk with me about important things like the wind and the honeybees. I love the animals and nature, but it's so nice to have like-minded human friends with whom I can share my dreams."

Traya agreed, "When I am with the boys from my village, I sometimes feel a little strange and different but, when I'm with you, everything feels right. It's like we see the world through one set of eyes, the way that all of the elephants and animals do."

"I think so too," said Asha.

"You know," said Traya, "if that woman on the bus in the big city had learnt to love herself for who she really is, she would have felt so much better. Anyway, what we look like changes as we get older." Traya laughed. "People are like the elephants—the older they get, the more wrinkles they have! At the end of the day," Traya mused mostly to himself, forgetting little Timba for a moment, "I guess it's up to us to choose which path to take through the forest. Some decisions will make us happy and some won't; and some people will keep changing, and some will get stuck."

"You sound so wise," said the young girl. "Thank you for the nice things you said about me."

"Nice things?" Traya wondered aloud. "Well, if I said nice things, Asha, it's because they are true. You are a special friend to me."

In response, she turned to Traya and gave him a great big hug.

"There," she said, "we are like the elephants now."

Chapter 14

Timba's Soft Eyes

Timba playfully sprayed them with water. Laughing freely, Traya gazed into the elephant calf's eyes. He imagined strings of golden light from his heart reaching into the heart of the elephant and offered his love. The baby elephant looked back, lifted its trunk onto Traya's lap and said, "Thank you for loving me."

Traya's eyes flashed with anger as he thought about the poachers who had killed the baby elephant's mother.

"Don't do that," called out the little one, wincing as if she had been pierced by a weapon.

"Don't do what?" Traya asked.

"Lash out with your sword of anger," replied Timba. "I accepted your love to help me, and you gave me more pain."

"I'm sorry," said Traya, "but I was angry at those poachers."

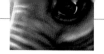

"You don't understand," said the little orphan, again moving closer to Traya. "When you send out anything but love, it hurts. Why do you think that elephants don't kill even though we are large and strong? Why is it that we eat only what Mother Earth gives freely? It is because we have chosen only to love. The elephants have roamed these lands for thousands of years in complete harmony, and the sound of our feet on the earth is the pulse of the Great Mother."

The little giant nuzzled her trunk against Traya's arm. "Should we become extinct, Mother Earth's power will start to fade. Already our numbers are dwindling and, with them, the balance and harmony of the earth is changing. We try to speak to the people through our soft eyes, but we are rarely heard. Please help your people to learn to love and not to take, to give and not to feel pity and, most of all, never to think of anger or send out hatred. Our survival and yours as a race depends on it.

"My mother was the matriarch of our herd, and she always knew where to go, when and why. When I'm older, it will become my responsibility to lead the others across the plains, keeping the song of the earth alive."

"How do you know so much?" asked Traya, in awe of the wisdom and directness of the tiny Timba.

"We are born knowing the truth," she replied. "We learn much in the womb of our mothers, for they teach us as they walk the land, pulsing power into the great earth with each step. They pull in air and light, the symphony of the stars, Surya's energy, and they send them down into the earth through their feet. As we grow in their wombs, we are part of this song of creation and part of this exchange of love. When we are born, our mothers teach us to see the light of creation in all things, through learning to see with soft eyes."

"Can I have soft eyes like yours?" Traya asked his young teacher.

"Yes, you can, because when you were growing in your mother's womb, you too became part of nature's symphony. Unfortunately, human civilisation puts the power of reason above instinct and natural intuition.

"You can find the soft eyes that still exist in your inner vision. You just need to reach into the fluid pool of your wisdom and let it find its own shape for every situation and circumstance. Just imagine you are not seeing with your eyes but from a place somewhere inside the back of your head."

Still sitting on the wall, Traya half closed his eyes, trying to see from the back of his head.

"Look through your eyes," said Timba, "soften your gaze, stop any judgment and just accept

what you see as beautiful and perfect. Try to see it as it truly is, without any part of you getting in the way."

Traya gazed gently at his wise, wrinkled little teacher with patches of red earth clinging to her fine hairs. Traya noticed the outlines of the little elephant beginning to fade.

"I think I'm getting it!" Traya exclaimed.

"Good," the elephant replied, "but stay gentle, and let your soul do the looking. Remember to send your love out of your eyes as well."

Traya felt himself softening inside, and a warm sense of connection and peace filled his heart. A smile began to play on his face, and a great energy began to rise up from his chest and shine out through his gaze.

"That's it. You've got it," exclaimed his little teacher.

"How can you tell?" asked Traya.

"I know because, when I look into your eyes, there is something coming out. Just as I felt your anger before, I can now feel your softness and kindness. What you think and feel comes out of you and becomes part of the world around us."

"What is coming out?" asked Traya excitedly.

"It is your soul-light, Traya," Timba said softly. "It's so powerful that it can heal, like Surya's rays, and, with that gaze, you can bring great light and love to others."

For a few precious moments more, Traya imagined himself also becoming a little elephant. The two played together in that place that has unlimited possibility and is without boundary or form.

Timba relished the innocent love pouring freely out of Traya's heart, and she opened her soul to its nourishing and healing powers. Eventually, Traya's meditation was broken by a little trunk touching his hand. Traya opened his eyes and reached out to stroke his new friend's head.

"Thank you," he said. "I will always love you." And for one huge moment, he gave his heart fearlessly and completely to a fellow being with whom he shared the earth.

"What happened?" asked Asha. She had been sitting quietly, watching the silent connection between her two friends, and she knew that something special and spiritual had happened.

"We talked about love," said Traya, "and soft eyes."

"I could feel it," she said. "It's like there was love in the air, and it was hugging me." That made Traya very happy.

Traya tilted his head back and, closing his eyes, filled his lungs with fresh afternoon air. When he opened his eyes to the heavens, he could see Surya over one shoulder between some fluffy white clouds, and Chandra was already making an early appearance, low in the sky over his other shoulder. They did not speak to him, but he could feel a silent message coming from the convergence of their rays and beams, as the light of day and night both shone on him at once. Then he looked into Asha's caring eyes and a new knowledge became clear to him.

"I understand now," he said as a small but deep smile grew on his face.

"Understand what?" asked Asha as she pulled a wildflower from the earth behind her and twirled the stem between her fingers and thumb. Then a honeybee gently alit on one of the petals.

"My *Dharma*. It's so simple. My *Dharma* is to give unconditional love all the time – and to give only love and nothing else."

"I'm here to give love to everyone and everything, just as Surya's *Dharma* is to give light during the day, Chandra's *Dharma* is to give light at night and the bees' *Dharma* is to give honey. And my gift allows me to let every one and every creature know of the unlimited love that all of nature wants to share with them."

"You're like an ambassador of love," Asha giggled, "translating messages of love that would otherwise never have been heard."

Traya grinned broadly and plucked another wildflower for Asha. "I think I came to meet Timba to learn about giving my heart in love without restraint. Perhaps, if all humans gave out kindness all the time, the world would be a better place."

Traya turned to Timba.

"Thank you," he said, hugging the neck of the powerful and now playful elephant. "You have helped me unlock the secret I've been looking for. I will always remember you and your lessons on love." Then he closed his eyes and chanted, "Ganesha Sharanam, Sharanam Ganesha."

Chapter 15

Kappo the Pigeon

Traya and Asha walked slowly away from the elephant enclosure towards the ranch house and found a place in the shade for a drink and an ice cream.

"All babies need a lot of love," Asha said. "My little sister is my reminder. If I don't play with her enough, she cries and cries."

"I guess, at birth, we forget that we are loved by all of creation," Traya agreed. "That must be the truth Timba talked of. We then spend the rest of our lives trying to remember that we are already made of love and that we still have the wisdom of the Great Spirit inside of us to guide us in using it."

"Sometimes I wish I were an animal," said Asha, "so I would always be able to love freely and know the right thing to do for Mother Earth."

"You don't have to be an animal, Asha," Traya said to his friend, with his new-found wisdom still flowing in his veins, "because you can learn from them every day. Look at that wasp over there. It knows it has a place in the heart of creation and is happy buzzing around, simply being

in love with life and itself. Last week, a wasp came to our kitchen for some sugar, and it told me about one of the ancient natural laws.

"The ancient law states that you always get what you think about and ask for from the universe," Traya went on. "The wasp only wants to collect sweet things to feed its nest of young, and so the the Universe freely gives it. The elephants want to be the pulse of the earth, so that is what they are. Surya and all the rest of creation come together to help all of us realise our thoughts and manifest our dreams.

"Then the wasp told me that, as humans, we are very unique and privileged, because we have choice. We can choose to be a bus driver or a musician, a doctor or a gardener, and we can work towards owning as much or as little as we like. The wasp said that all the forces around us would then help us to achieve that which we seek."

"What do you seek?" the girl asked Traya.

"Well, I think I want to live my *Dharma* and be happy," Traya replied, sipping his juice and licking the ice cream. "I know a house is important to keep us safe, and a job will bring in money to buy food, but if we grow up thinking that's it, then we will have missed finding out what we came here to do."

A pigeon landed nearby, hoping to have some scraps of lunch tossed her way. Traya looked at

the bird, and threw some of his ice cream cone towards her. She hopped closer and pecked away, watching the two young children considering their lives.

"Hi," she said to Traya, "I'm called Kappo, and I couldn't help but overhear your conversation. Do you mind if I add something?"

"Go ahead." Traya nodded to the bird, which was pecking at the grass.

"Well, some time ago, my partner and I had a real fright when some of our young got caught in a hunter's net."

"I'm sorry to hear that," Traya said.

"They were very lucky," Kappo the pigeon chirped. "We managed to free them just in time, but we almost got caught in the process."

"Are they still free?" asked Traya, keen to know the rest of the story.

"Oh, yes, and they have gone off traveling to see other lands and meet other birds. But it made me realise how precious life is, and how short it could have been. We all get so caught up in trivial things, we forget the most important things in life, like our *Dharma* and doing what is essential."

"What is your *Dharma*?" Traya asked Kappo, who was now sitting on Traya's knee and wiping her beak on his shorts.

"Don't you know?" she asked Traya, seeming quite surprised.

"Er…no," Traya admitted.

"That's strange," Kappo said. "How about you?" she asked the girl. "Do you know what my *Dharma* is?"

Traya had to be the interpreter and asked Asha, "Do you know what birds do, what makes them and the entire universe happy?"

"No, I've never thought about it," she said, quite used to Traya's strange conversations with the animals and birds.

Traya looked down at Kappo and said, "No, we have never thought about it."

"There's part of the problem." The bird hopped along Traya's leg, somewhat annoyed. "You don't ask the question, so the answer will not come to you."

"The wasp said almost the same thing," said Traya, interrupting the flow of conversation.

"Exactly!" Kappo sighed. "The natural laws don't seem to be taught to the fledgling humans anymore. Still, I can tell you two, and you can pass it on. The *Dharma* of the birds," she said puffing out her chest, "is to sing to the plants and make them grow. We do a very good job of it!" she added with a wink.

"Birdsong is very beautiful," Traya added, trying to regain some dignity, "but I didn't know it was so important."

"Well, now you do," said the pigeon, hopping onto the ground and turning to look at Traya. "We sing, and green things grow. We hear Surya's tune, which comes with his first morning light, and pass it on to the plant kingdom. Take us away and they would really struggle.

"I guess you could call it a love song," she added, chirping happily to herself. "We have favourite plants, of course, but we sing to all the plants because they all need our love. It's a simple thing: love, song, earth, light, water, and then everything stays in harmony. It's called the dawn chorus."

"Wow," said Traya, who had been translating to his friend as the pigeon chatted away. "That's amazing. I never knew the importance of the birds and their connection. I'll make sure I feed the birds every day for the rest of my life," he promised, quite moved by the interconnectedness of everything he was learning.

"Who needs to learn natural history from a book?" he laughed. "I'm getting it all here in nature. Thanks," he said to Kappo, who was now finishing Asha's ice cream cone.

"You're welcome!" she said and flew onto a nearby branch. "And remember. Don't be caught up in the many unimportant things. Keep your mind on the bigger picture!" Then off she flew into the sky.

Chapter 16

The Fire Speaks

Traya and the girl sat in silence for a while, trying to absorb the amazing amount of knowledge passed on to them that day. Asha looked at Traya.

"So, do you really think your *Dharma* is as simple as giving love, Traya?"

Traya nodded slowly and took a deep breath. "I think that is the essence of all *Dharmas*, really, Asha. It's more about the way we go about doing it. Whether it is singing like the birds or teaching like my mother or making honey or caring for the sick, we must all find our special place in the chain of love that brings joy and healing and purpose to the universe. My *Dharma* is to give love day and night," said Traya, "and to use my gift to allow all beings and elements to share it. I know it now and if ever I forget, all I have to do is look around at all my friends in nature to remember who I am and what I'm here for. What about you, Asha?"

"I'm still thinking about it," she said. "I can feel a little voice inside my heart telling me to love and care for animals. When I grow up, I know I will want to teach my children and others all the things we are learning about the powers of Mother Earth. But let's see what happens. I can't hear

all the words of the animals as you can, Traya, but as long as I'm here in the wild, I can feel the little voices all around, guiding me and loving me. If I lose that connection as a grown up, I will return to nature to find it, just as you said you would do."

Traya and Asha stood up and hugged each other.

"I have to go now," he said, "or it will be too dark and dangerous to go home."

"Why not stay here tonight, and come to see the rhinos tomorrow?"

"I wish I could, but I can't," said Traya, who had been out with Asha and her father before and loved it. "My folks will worry. Is it ok to come next week to join you for an adventure then? We might see some lions and giraffes."

"It's been a great day," Asha said, not wanting Traya to leave, as he had brought with him such wisdom and real, uncomplicated friendship.

"Until we meet again," he finally said to break the silence, "let's practise having soft eyes." He smiled at his friend, and turned to begin the long jog home, feeling very much as though he were leaving a part of himself behind. Traya was fit and light, both in body and heart, and by running he could be home in half the time.

That night, as his thoughts turned to Asha and Timba, Traya stroked the sleeping Py and put Papilio on a creeper by the door. After supper, he sat by the fire and thought about his last few days. The fire crackled and hissed as a piece of damp wood rolled over in the embers. Traya gazed at the flames, which looked so much like a miniature Surya.

"Thank you for your warmth," he said, mesmerised by the dancing figures. The Fire sparked and spit in reply, and Traya listened, his eyes locked into the centre of the flames.

"Thank you, Traya," it crackled back, "for being so happy and free and for learning so much. Remember, Traya, that not everyone will understand you, or ever get to know you fully. Some people will pick up a piece of wood and see my fire within it, and some won't. Some will meet you and see the wisdom and love you have to offer the world, and some won't. Know that now, and you won't be disappointed in life."

Traya smiled as he felt the warm love of the Fire's *Dharma* reflected back to him.

"Keep your inner fire of love stoked up," the Fire added, "but don't be offended when you meet those who appear to reject it. Be like me, Traya, a living flame for those who seek the light of truth."

"I'll try," Traya replied. "I really enjoy learning from all of try. It's so exciting, and there is always something new to explore and hear about."

Suddenly, the fire cracked loudly four times, each time sending six sparks toward Traya and a spark of insight into his mind.

"Just think…I have had at least 24 teachers in the past few days." Counting on his fingers, he listed his guides and teachers. "There was Mama,, the Flamingos, Surya the sun, Mother Earth, Vayu Wind, Yamuna River, Varuna the Ocean and Chandra the moon. Then there was the Sky, Papilio, Pythagoras, the Fish in Py's story, the Deer, the Little People and the Spider. And I learned from the Beekeeper, my friend Asha and the Woman on the bus. I also learned from the Honeybees, Russell, the injured Squirrel, Timba, the Wasp and the Pigeon."

"That's only 23!" the Fire teased him. "You have miscounted."

"No," laughed Traya, "I've not forgotten one of man's best and oldest friends."

"Who's that?" The Fire sparkled, as he loved mysteries and suspense.

"You!" said Traya, giving him a poke. And the two of them roared with laughter. Fire leaped up as high as he could go, and threw out a huge spark to make Traya jump.

Ana came into the room and saw Traya in a fit of laughter.

"Come on now! It's time for bed." She pushed Traya's shoulder lightly towards his bedroom,

and gently placed some logs on the Fire.

"There, that should keep you happy overnight," she said, and the Fire calmed down.

"See you in the morning," he mumbled, with his mouth full of some spongy bark. "I'll have your porridge hot for you when you wake up."

"Sweet dreams," Traya called to the Fire, as he turned to head for his little bed. "What a wonderful day," he yawned. "I wonder what secrets will unfold for me tomorrow?" With that, Traya slipped below the mosquito net under his old worn blanket and went to sleep.

The End

Paulette Agnew

Paulette is an exuberant lover of wild and natural places. She has explored the mysteries of conscious awakening and ancient spiritual truths. Her curiosity and adventurous lifestyle are driven by her quest to uncover the answers to life's big questions about herself and the human condition.

Born of rock-climbing and mountaineering parents, and growing up in Cumbria and Scotland, she spent every spare moment outdoors. Often grubby, barefoot and left to run free or go exploring on horseback, her formative years were dictated by the seasons, raw nature and the animals around her. In her Traya series, Paulette translates her experiences, visions and perceptions through the eyes of a young boy growing up in the Rift Valley of Kenya.

For Paulette, the path of developing conscious Awareness was never something to be found on the TV or movie screen, but in the remarkable earthly paradise that was her backyard.

Much like her little hero, Traya, she did most of her learning in the arena of life. Eventually, however, at age 8, she picked up a book and fell in love with reading, which became another source to quench her thirst for knowledge and understanding.

Paulette's openness and inquisitiveness carry over to her love of learning and into her own writing style. She often finds knowledge and wisdom that are too close, too personal or too small for the ordinary person to even notice. Filling up her heart from this unique perspective, she lets the insights and imaginative stories flow onto the page, more like a photograph developing in a tray of chemicals than sentences being constructed.

An Honours degree in Biochemistry at Manchester University sparked a lifelong love of how the human body works. Science never replaced, but rather augmented, her love of nature and mysticism.

She spent six years teaching the art of survival training, bushcraft and vision quests in the wilderness, and has spent time in ashrams. Her life is a continuous study of the unseen and eternal, practising daily yoga, meditation and pranayama. She loves to read ancient texts like the *Srimad Bhagavatam and the Vedas* and has traveled many times to India. Paulette shares these skills with her students in her yoga and meditation teacher training courses.

She worked with the UNHCR (UN Refugee Agency), the USAID and the US Embassy in Kenya, running trauma healing programs and rehabilitation of child soldiers in Southern Sudan's war zones. This sat well alongside her love of safaris, the red earth of Africa and camping under the vast canopy of the night sky.

Paulette is also an award-winning inspirational speaker for Vistage, helping CEOs bring balance into their lives while maintaining high performance outcomes. She is a mentor, motivator and visionary, who enjoys sharing her accumulated insights through the spoken and written word.

Her life's aim is to deepen her compassion, forgiveness and humility, whilst sharing universal spiritual knowledge hidden in our everyday experiences. But, if there is a fun adventure to be had, Paulette will be there!

You can learn more about Paulette and Traya by visiting trayasquest.com or contact her at: paulette@trayasquest.com

Find her on Traya's Quest Facebook and discuss your favourite teachers, life lessons and share your own quests and adventures. www.facebook/trayasquest